SNOW TROLL

Margaret McAllister

Illustrated by

Steve Co

OXFORI
UNIVERSITY PRESS

OXFORD
UNIVERSITY PRESS

Great Clarendon Street, Oxford, OX2 6DP,
United Kingdom

Oxford University Press is a department of the University of Oxford.
It furthers the University's objective of excellence in research, scholarship,
and education by publishing worldwide. Oxford is a registered trade mark of
Oxford University Press in the UK and in certain other countries

First published in this edition 2018

British Library Cataloguing in Publication Data
Data available

978-0-19-276527-7

1 3 5 7 9 10 8 6 4 2

Paper used in the production of this book is a natural, recyclable product
made from wood grown in sustainable forests. The manufacturing process
conforms to the environmental regulations of the country of origin.

Printed in China

Acknowledgements

Cover and inside illustrations by Steve Cox
Background images by Shutterstock
Series editor: Alison Sage

For Peter Hood

Helping your child to read

Before they start

- Talk about the back cover blurb. How might a troll be able to help people?
- Look at the front cover. What would your child think if they saw a troll like Tromso?

During reading

- Let your child read at their own pace – don't worry if it's slow. They could read silently, or read to you out loud.
- Help them to work out words they don't know by saying each sound out loud and then blending them to say the word, e.g. *d-r-ea-d-f-u-l, dreadful.*
- If your child still struggles with a word, just tell them the word and move on.
- Give them lots of praise for good reading!

After reading

- Look at page 32 for some fun activities.

Chapter One

Tromso was a tame troll. He lived in a village called Hoppings, at the bottom of a mountain. He was grey and very big.

Everybody liked Tromso. He was very helpful. If anybody asked, he would cut down a tree. Or build a wall.

To thank him, people gave him things to eat. What he liked most were cakes, bananas, bricks, cabbages, old chair legs and jigsaw puzzles with pieces missing.

Tromso kept everything. He used the things to mend his house, and if he was hungry, he ate them.

Peter and Joy were Tromso's friends. Joy was Peter's sister.

One morning, Tromso was at their house when the postman came.

Tromso saw the letters drop through the letterbox.

"What are those?" asked Tromso.

"Letters," said Peter.

Tromso found the letters very interesting.

When he went home, he made a letterbox in his front door.

All the next day and the day after that, Tromso stayed at home. Peter saw him at the window and went to see him.

Tromso was sitting sadly on the floor, eating a brick.

"My letterbox doesn't work," said Tromso. "I made a letterbox to get letters! But they don't come."

"Oh, Tromso!" said Peter. "Somebody has to *send* you the letters!"

Peter ran home and wrote a letter. He put his letter in an envelope, stuck on a stamp, and posted it.

The next day, Tromso came to Peter's house. He was grinning.

"I got a letter!" he said.

"Good!" said Peter. "Have you read it?"

Tromso looked upset.

"I can't read," he said, sadly.

"I'll read it for you," said Joy.
The letter said:

Dear Tromso,

Your new letterbox works!

Mum says you can have tea at our house today.

Love, Peter xxx

"I wish I could read," said Tromso.
"I know!" said Peter. "We'll teach you."
"Yes, please!" said Tromso.

Everyone in Hoppings helped Tromso.
They put up signs in the village.

Bit by bit, Tromso learned to read.
He even learned to write his name.
But he took care not to eat the pencils.

Chapter Two

One morning, a bright blue envelope fell through Tromso's letterbox.

There was a card inside. Tromso read it all by himself.

"Come to my birthday party at three o'clock on Saturday! Love, Peter."

Tromso was puzzled. He went to Peter and Joy's house.

“I read my letter,” Tromso said.

“Didn’t it make you happy?” said Peter.

“I don’t understand,” said Tromso. “There are hard words in it. I know Sunday and Monday and those days. What is ‘birthday’?”

Peter told him about birthdays and parties.

"When is your birthday, Tromso?" he said.

"I've never had one," said Tromso sadly.

"You can share mine," said Peter. "We'll share a party. Mum always makes a cake for birthdays. I'll ask her to make one for you."

“How does she make cakes?” asked Tromso.

“She mixes up lots of nice things,” said Peter. “Then she puts sweets and candles on top.”

That gave Tromso an idea.

Tromso looked in his junk heap for things he liked to eat.

He found pebbles, old chairs, string and sand. He stirred them up with plenty of glue. Then he put everything in the sun to dry.

It was even bigger than Tromso, and it didn't look like a cake. So he put sugar and chopped cabbage and a very big candle on top. That was better.

On Peter and Tromso's birthday, everyone gave them presents.

There were even some things for Tromso to eat, like an old shopping basket and a dead tree.

They played Pass the Parcel.
Tromso ate the wrapping paper.

They played chase.
Tromso fell in the duck pond.

They played Hide and Seek.
Tromso was too big to hide anywhere.

Then Peter and Joy handed round birthday cake.

"Surprise!" said Tromso. He showed everyone his cake.

"It looks very nice," said Peter. But it didn't. Nobody wanted to eat it.

Then Peter had an idea.

"That cake is too special to eat," he said.

"Is it as good as *that?*" said Tromso.

"We'll keep it outside," said Joy. "We could play on it."

"It's a very strong cake," said Tromso. "It won't break if you climb on it."

So they put the cake beside the duck pond. Everyone played on it.

Peter put up a notice:

Tromso was very happy.

The children loved Tromso's cake, and nobody minded if Tromso took a bite out of it now and again!

Chapter Three

In winter, snow fell on Hoppings. The mountain was sparkling white.

The children built a huge snowman. It was their best snowman ever.

It snowed again, and the snow came to the top of Joy's boots. She gave the snowman a hat.

It didn't stop snowing.

Peter's mum looked at the mountain.

"I hope it stops snowing," she said.

"Why?" asked Peter.

"Because there could be an avalanche," she said. "An avalanche is very dangerous. The snow gets heavier and heavier and slides down the mountain."

But it didn't stop snowing.

Everyone asked Tromso, "Will you help us to clear away the snow?"

"All of it?" said Tromso.

"Yes please," they said. "But don't get cold."

"Trolls don't feel the cold," said Tromso.

He took a big spade. He cleared away heaps of snow. Then he saw the snowman.

"It's a pity to spoil it," he said. "But they told me to clear away the snow, and a snowman is made of snow." He put the hat on a gatepost. Then he cleared up the snowman with his spade.

Soon, the children came out to play. "Where is our snowman?" they cried.

Everyone was very cross when they saw that Tromso had knocked it down. Tromso felt dreadful.

Peter and Joy found Tromso at the bottom of the mountain. A big tear ran down Tromso's face and melted a hole in the snow. Joy hugged him.

Just then, they heard a low, rumbling sound. Something on the mountain was moving.

Snow! It was an avalanche!

"Help!" yelled Peter.
"We must warn everyone!"

Peter and Joy ran to the village.

"Avalanche!" they shouted.

Everyone ran.

Tromso stood still and held out his arms.

"I don't know if I can stop an avalanche," he said. "But I can try."

Snow rolled faster and faster down the mountain in a huge snowball.

Rumble, rumble, went the snowball, as it grew bigger and bigger.

"Run, Tromso!" shouted Joy.

Tromso didn't move.

The snowball landed on Tromso.

"Oof!" said Tromso.

The snowball rolled a bit more, then stopped.

The snowball got up. It had troll feet and troll hands. It had Tromso's face smiling out at the top.